The JOURNEY of the MARMABILL

Daniel Errico

Illustrations by Tiffany Turrill

Sky Pony Press
New York

Sky Pony Press books may be purchased in bulk at special discounts for sales promotion,
corporate gifts, fund-raising, or educational purposes. Special editions can also be
created to specifications. For details, contact the Special Sales Department, Sky Pony
Press, 307 West 36th Street, 11th Floor, New York, NY 10018 or
info@skyhorsepublishing.com.

Sky Pony® is a registered trademark of Skyhorse Publishing, Inc.®, a Delaware
corporation.

Visit our website at www.skyponypress.com.

10 9 8 7 6 5 4 3 2

Library of Congress Cataloging-in-Publication Data is available on file.

ISBN: 978-1-62087-736-4

Manufactured in China, April 2020
This product conforms to CPSIA 2008

To the Hero

A marmabill was searching on the rainy forest floor.
She came up to a tree that had a tiny wooden door.

She'd traveled very far and where she was, she didn't know.

She'd never been so scared and wasn't sure which way to go.

She gave a gentle knock and twenty
    wugs came rolling out.

When wugs hear any noise, they want
    to see what it's about.

"I'm looking for a creature. He has
    run off with my nest,

But now I've lost my way, and I could use a place to rest."

"If he has come this way, I'm sure you'll find him on this path.

But we have beds and lots of food and sniff, oh my, a bath!"

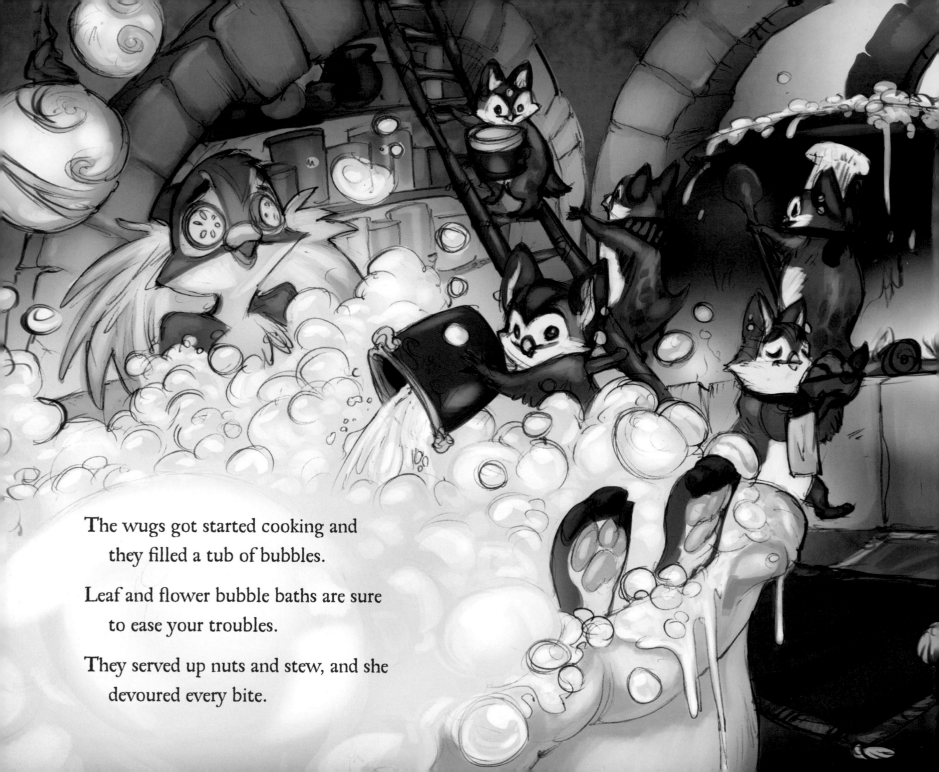

The wugs got started cooking and
they filled a tub of bubbles.

Leaf and flower bubble baths are sure
to ease your troubles.

They served up nuts and stew, and she
devoured every bite.

And played some Toss-the-Wug
until they fell asleep
mid-flight!

"Please don't go!" they pleaded, when she
thanked them for her stay.

She said, "I may still be lost, but I am on
my way."

The marmabill walked over logs and under heavy brush.

Her tiny legs were moving fast, like she was in a rush.

She stopped for just a moment by a lazy flowing river,

And ate some berry snacks the wugs were nice enough to give her.

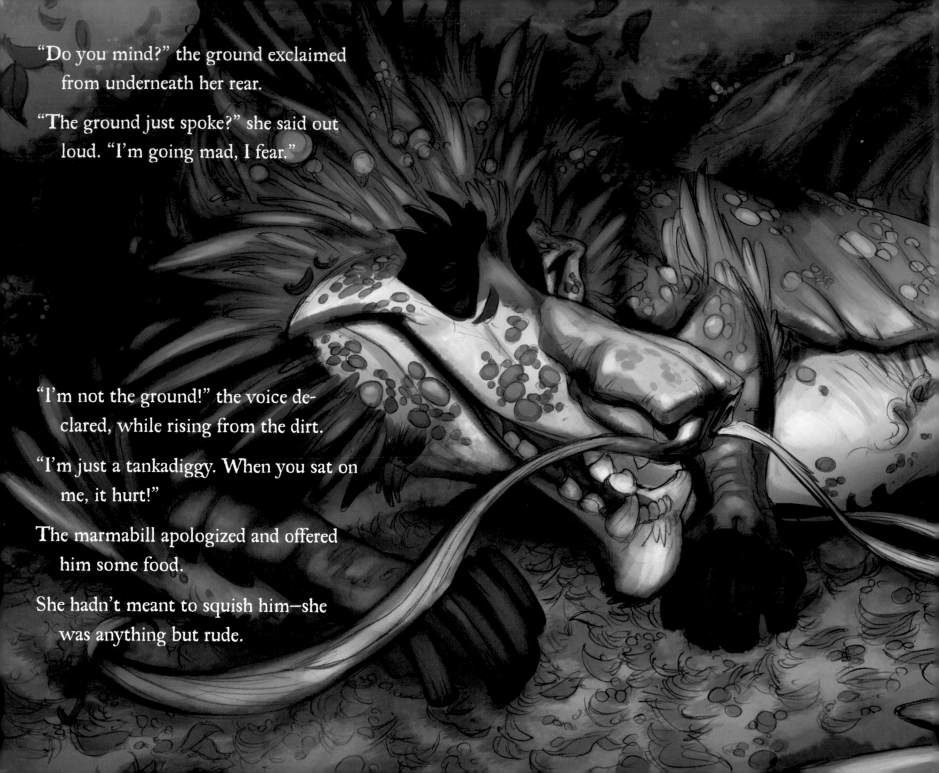

"Do you mind?" the ground exclaimed
from underneath her rear.

"The ground just spoke?" she said out
loud. "I'm going mad, I fear."

"I'm not the ground!" the voice de-
clared, while rising from the dirt.

"I'm just a tankadiggy. When you sat on
me, it hurt!"

The marmabill apologized and offered
him some food.

She hadn't meant to squish him—she
was anything but rude.

"I'm looking for my home," she said, and
    he responded, "Why?"

"A buldabeast has taken it!" Then she
    began to cry.

"I saw one pass me by and he was carrying
    a sack."

"I knew it!" said the marmabill, "I've
    gotten back on track!"

Following the river, she went far
along the bank,

But did not see the key-keys who
had set a nasty prank.

She fell inside a hole that they had
covered up with plants.

They chuckled from the trees, while
building stacks of olly ants.

She slipped along a muddy slide that
traveled underground.

And when it stopped, the marmabill
was all mixed up around.

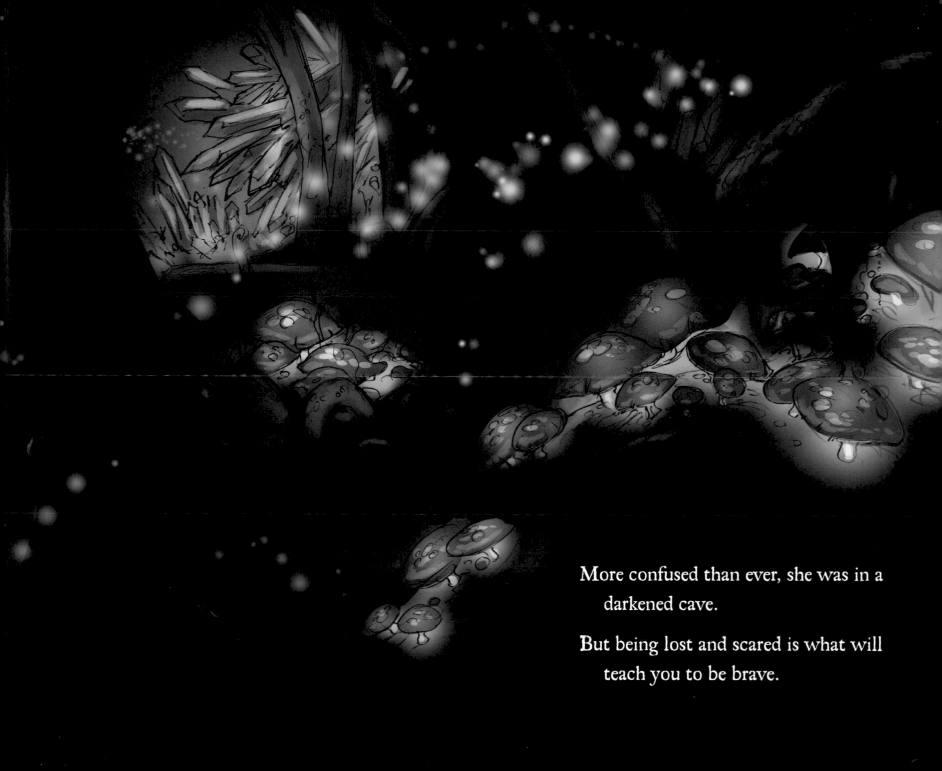

More confused than ever, she was in a darkened cave.

But being lost and scared is what will teach you to be brave.

She couldn't see a thing, but she could
hear as well as ever,

Which gave her an idea that was as odd
as it was clever.

She grabbed a bunch of rocks, and
threw them here and there.

And when they hit a wall or dip, the
sound would tell her where.

She walked along, until she threw a
rock up to the ceiling.

It made a funny sound that gave her
quite a scary feeling.

Instead of hitting stone, she'd hit a soundly
 sleeping fluther.

Soon its eyes lit up and started waking up
 another.

One hundred fluthers fluttered down, glowing
 emerald green.

Having just been woken, they were acting
 cranky and mean!

They chased her down a tunnel 'til
she ended up outside.

A fluther pulled her by the tail and
took her for a ride.

She grabbed a branch while flying by
and managed to break free,

And found herself on top of a
Bonondabonza tree.

"I see him!" said the marmabill. "That
thieving buldabeast!"

He sat beneath a waterfall she spotted
to the east.

She grabbed the nearest vine and started swinging through the air.

But when she reached the buldabeast he gave an icy stare.

"Give me back my nest!"
she yelled in quite a
shaky voice.

She may have been afraid,
but she had made a
mighty choice.

The buldabeast came charging. He was in a foul mood.

(Buldabeasts are known to have a fiery attitude.)

When she looked for cover it was then she recognized,

That she was near a key-key trap, cleverly disguised.

As she jumped away, the buldabeast went running by.

He fell into the trap, and he was hoisted to the sky.

"Let me down!" he shouted, as he dangled from the net.

"You stole my home," she answered, "and now this is what you get."

Her nest was trampled underfoot, but she knew
what to do.

After all she'd done, she wasn't scared to start
anew.

She started finding twigs and built a new home
that made her proud.

Wugs and key-keys welcome, but no
buldabeasts allowed!